MW01252647

Capstone Short Biographies

Women in Chemistry Careers

by Jetty Kahn

Consultant:
David Lewis, Ph.D.
Professor of Chemistry
University of Wisconsin, Eau Claire

CAPSTONE BOOKS
an imprint of Capstone Press
Mankato, Minnesota

Capstone Books are published by Capstone Press
818 North Willow Street, Mankato, MN 56001
http://www.capstone-press.com

Library of Congress Cataloging-in-Publication Data
Kahn, Jetty.
  Women in chemistry careers/by Jetty Kahn.
  p. cm.—(Capstone short biographies)
  Includes bibliographical references and index.
  Summary: Describes the careers of five women working in the field of
chemistry: Ann Crespi, Molly Fiedler, Linda Griffith, Lynda Jordan, and
Malathy Nair.
  ISBN 0-7368-0315-7
  1. Women chemists—United States—Biography—Juvenile literature.
[1. Chemists. 2. Women Biography.] I. Title. II. Series.
QD21.K26 2000
540'.92'273—DC21   99-22297
                                                                         CIP

Editorial Credits
Connie R. Colwell, editor, Timothy Halldin, cover designer; Heidi Schoof,
  photo researcher

Photo Credits
Ann Crespi, cover, 10
Barbara Peacock/FPG International LLC, 27
Index Stock Imagery, 6, 24
International Stock/Patrick Ramsey, 4
Linda Griffith, 22
Lynda Jordan, 28, 30
Malathy Nair, 34, 40
Molly Fiedler, 16, 19, 20
Photo Network/Paul Thompson, 38
Uniphoto, 8, 13, 33, 37, 47
Visuals Unlimited/Ned Therrien, 14

Table of Contents

Chapter 1

Chemistry

Chemistry is the study of chemicals. These substances make up all things on the earth. Chemicals can be natural or artificial. Natural chemicals exist in the air, water, and land. Artificial chemicals are made by people. These chemicals are used in making things such as medicines, plastic, and cloth.

Scientists who study chemicals are called chemists. Chemists study how chemicals act and react with each other. They also study how chemicals change from one form to another. For example, sugar changes into caramel when it is heated.

Chemists study how chemicals act and react with each other.

Many chemists do research in laboratories.

Some chemists combine chemicals to create new materials. These chemists may make plastics, soaps, medicines, and other materials from chemicals.

Chemistry Fields
Chemists work in several different areas. These areas are called fields. Some chemists work with the environment. Chemists in this field

may study the way chemicals react with nature. They may find ways to clean up air and water.

Other chemists work in the medical field. These chemists may study how people's bodies react to certain chemicals. They may create new medicines from chemicals. They may use chemistry to create machines that help sick people. Medicinal chemists may work to create medicines to help cure diseases.

Chemists also work in other fields. Some chemists study the earth. These chemists may try to learn how life started on the earth. Other chemists design household products. They may create products such as soaps and lotions.

Many chemists do research. Research is the study of one subject. Chemists do research in many ways. They read the latest information about their research subject. They also perform experiments to learn more about the subject.

Chemists do research in laboratories. These rooms have special equipment that chemists use for experiments. Laboratories often are

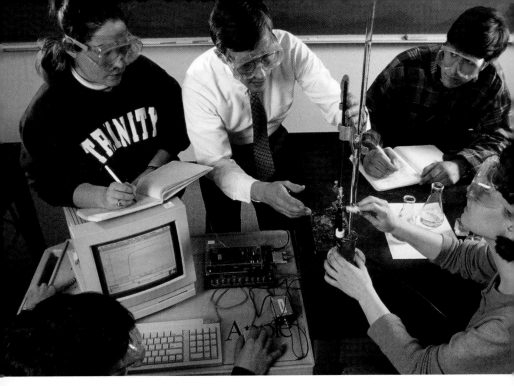

People who want to be chemists must attend a college or university.

located in universities, government buildings, or manufacturing businesses.

Education
People who want to be chemists should have certain personal qualities and skills. People who like to do experiments often make good chemists. These people usually are curious.

They often enjoy experimenting to create new chemical mixtures.

People who want to be chemists must attend a college or university. They must take classes in chemistry and other sciences. College students earn a bachelor's degree after completing a course of study at a university or college. People can complete a bachelor's degree in about four years.

Many chemists find jobs after they earn a bachelor's degree. Chemists with bachelor's degrees may teach in elementary or high schools. They may design products for chemical companies or do other work in a chemistry field.

Some chemists go on to earn a master's or doctoral degree. Doctoral degrees are the most advanced degrees available from universities. Chemists who earn doctoral degrees may teach at universities or colleges. They may do research and perform experiments in university or manufacturing laboratories. Chemists with doctoral degrees have other related career opportunities as well.

Chapter 2
Ann Crespi

Ann Crespi enjoys in-line skating. This exercise helps her heart stay healthy and strong. But some people do not have healthy hearts. Crespi uses her skills as a chemist to help these people lead normal lives.

Crespi's education helped prepare her for a career as a chemist. She earned a bachelor's degree from Yale University in New Haven, Connecticut. She later earned a doctoral degree in chemistry from Northwestern University in Evanston, Illinois.

Today, Crespi is a chemist at Medtronic in Minneapolis, Minnesota. Medtronic is one of

Ann Crespi is a chemist at Medtronic in Minneapolis, Minnesota.

the largest medical companies in the world. At Medtronic, Crespi designs machines to help people with unhealthy hearts.

ICDs

The heart pumps blood to all parts of the body. The body needs this blood to live. Accidents and heart attacks can cause the heart to beat too quickly. The heart then stops pumping blood to some parts of the body. People can die if the heart does not continue to pump blood properly.

But these accidents and heart attacks are not always fatal. Doctors sometimes can make a person's heart pump properly again. Doctors use special machines to shock a heart that is not beating properly. The shock forces the heart to beat properly again.

A heart may not heal completely after an accident or heart attack. People with damaged hearts may need occasional shocks to keep their hearts working properly.

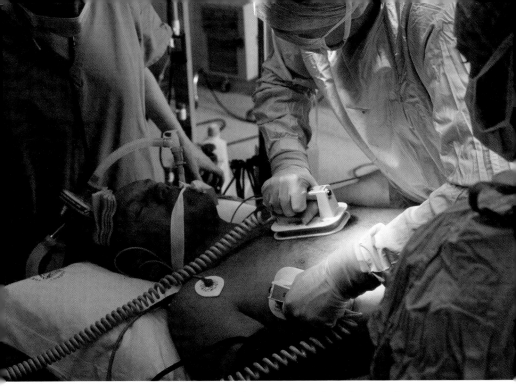

Doctors use a special machine to shock a heart that is not beating properly.

Doctors use machines to help damaged hearts continue to beat properly. These machines are called implantable cardioverter defibrillators (ICDs). Doctors operate to place an ICD inside a person's chest. The ICD gives an occasional shock to a person's heart. These shocks are quick, powerful, and sometimes painful. But the shocks help a person's heart beat properly at all times.

ICDs do not shock a person's heart when the person performs exercises such as hiking.

Crespi designs batteries and capacitors for ICDs. Capacitors take energy from the batteries. They use the energy to shock the heart. This allows the heart to pump blood to other parts of the body.

An ICD only shocks a person's heart when the heart beats uncontrollably. A person's heartbeat usually increases gradually with emotional or physical stress. ICDs do not give shocks when heartbeats gradually get faster.

People do not get shocked when they hurry to answer the phone or go for long hikes.

Crespi uses her chemistry skills to design smaller ICDs. Today, ICDs are about the size of a computer disk. Crespi experiments with different substances used to make ICDs. These substances include metal, plastic, and clay. ICDs made from these substances may fit more easily inside people's chests.

Other Medical Machines

Crespi also designs batteries for other medical machines. One of these machines is the cardiac pacemaker. Pacemakers are similar to ICDs. Pacemakers help hearts beat properly. But they help people whose hearts beat too slowly or out of rhythm. People of all ages can have pacemakers installed in their chests. Even some newborns have pacemakers.

Crespi works to improve medical machines. She travels around the United States. She meets with other researchers and doctors to find ways to make better medical machines. Crespi's work may help save many lives each year.

Chapter 3
Molly Fiedler

Molly Fiedler enjoys looking for herbs, spices, and flowers with interesting smells. As a chemist, she uses these materials to create scented products in a laboratory.

Fiedler's education helped prepare her for a career as a chemist. She earned a bachelor's degree in chemistry at Hamline University in St. Paul, Minnesota.

Today, she works for a fragrance company in Minneapolis, Minnesota. She also studies business administration. She hopes skills in business will help her with the job of designing and selling scented products.

Molly Fiedler uses chemistry to make scented products.

Polymers

Fiedler studied chemical compounds called polymers at Hamline. These substances are made of small parts linked together in long chains. Plastic is a polymer. A company called Minnesota Mining and Manufacturing (3M) hired Fiedler to work with polymers. She began making small cases for perfume samples in magazines.

Fiedler used polymers to make these perfume sample cases. She placed perfume inside tiny capsules. These small cases then were placed in glue. The glue made the capsules stick inside magazines. People broke the capsules open when they touched or scratched them. This released the perfume.

Fiedler worked with other polymers at 3M. She experimented with polymer substances to make scented color crayons. Fiedler's first crayons smelled like fruit. But some children ate these crayons. Fiedler then made crayons that smelled like pine trees.

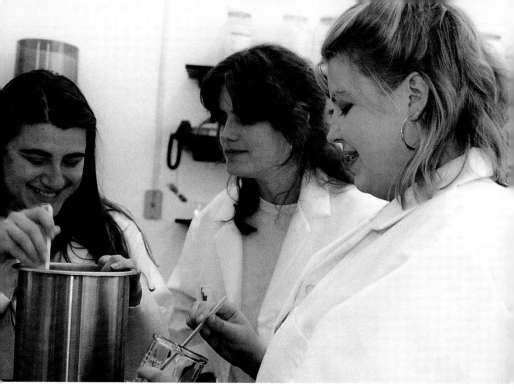

Molly Fiedler (right) works with other scientists to create scented products.

Scented Products

Today, Fiedler works for The Thymes Limited. This company makes and sells scented products. Fiedler makes lotions, soaps, and shampoos. She also makes candles, sprays, and potpourri. People keep this mixture of flowers, herbs, and spices in a jar and use it for scent.

The products Molly Fiedler creates are not tested on animals.

Fiedler spends much of her time in a laboratory. She works with a biologist and a food scientist to make scented products. The biologist makes sure Fiedler's products do not have germs in them. The food scientist studies how scents make people feel. For example, the smells of some flowers relax people. Other smells make people feel happy. Fiedler wants to make products that affect people in good ways.

Some companies test their new products on animals. But many people object to testing products on animals. They believe such tests mistreat animals. The products Fiedler creates are not tested on animals. People offer to test the new products instead.

Fiedler has other duties at The Thymes Limited. Her training in business administration sometimes helps her with these duties. She often writes descriptions of new items for company advertising. Fiedler's descriptions must be interesting and accurate. They should encourage people to buy the products.

Fiedler also studies comments from customers. These comments help her understand what customers want. Fiedler then can find better ways to make and sell scented products.

Chapter 4
Linda Griffith

As a college student, Linda Griffith visited sick children in a hospital. She became interested in making these children well. She studied and trained in chemistry to accomplish that goal.

Griffith earned a doctoral degree in chemical engineering from the University of California in Berkeley. Chemical engineers use chemistry to design new items.

Today, Griffith works at the Massachusetts Institute of Technology (MIT) in Cambridge, Massachusetts. She creates artificial body organs. These organs are not natural. But they

Linda Griffith creates artificial body organs at the Massachusetts Institute of Technology (MIT).

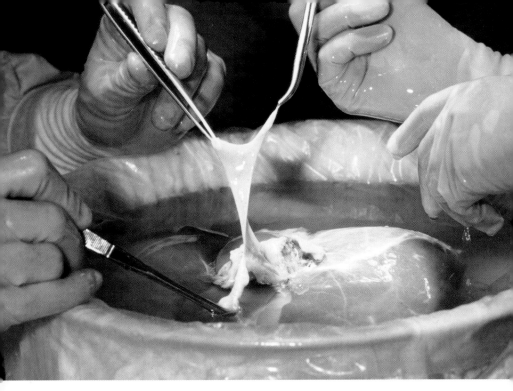

Medical scientists prepare donors' livers for transplant into people with unhealthy livers.

work like natural organs. Griffith hopes to save people's lives by making artificial organs to replace unhealthy ones.

Children's Hospital

Griffith first became interested in artificial organs when she visited Children's Hospital in Boston, Massachusetts. There, she met many sick children. These children had unhealthy organs. They needed transplants to replace their unhealthy organs with healthy ones.

24

Children who need transplants must have organ donors. These people give part or all of one of their own organs to another person. Organ transplants can save children's lives.

Many of the patients at Children's Hospital needed new livers. Healthy livers perform many tasks. The liver cleans the blood. It stores and digests fat. The liver helps heal wounds. It also helps create waste materials. Some of the children received liver transplants. But many of the children died before donors could be found.

Griffith began to design artificial livers that worked like natural livers. She hoped the artificial livers could replace unhealthy natural livers. The children then would not need donors for transplants. The artificial livers could save children's lives.

Artificial Livers

Livers are made of cells. Liver cells can grow quickly. Griffith wanted to try to grow an artificial liver from a few liver cells. These cells needed a special place to grow.

Griffith created a place for the liver cells to grow. She made a spongy case about the size of a dime. Liver cells could grow and feed inside this case.

Griffith also found a way to group the cells into one organ. She attached tiny plastic strings inside the spongy case. The strings held the cells together into a whole liver. But this liver still was very small.

In the future, scientists will test these small livers in rats and dogs with liver problems. Scientists hope to see if the artificial livers work safely. Soon, Griffith hopes to make artificial livers about the size of a lemon. These livers may be able to function inside people. Griffith hopes her work someday will save many lives.

Scientists hope to save many lives with artificial livers.

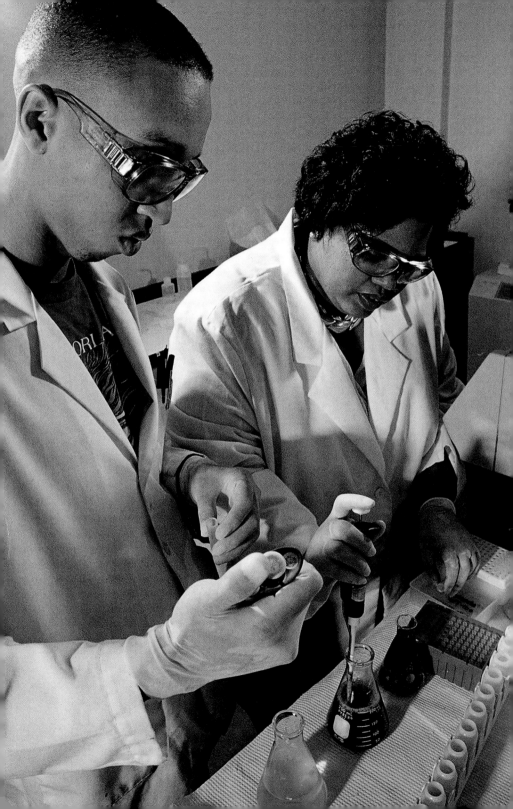

Chapter 5
Lynda Jordan

Lynda Jordan enjoys singing and dancing. She knows that healthy lungs help people sing and dance. But some people have a disease called asthma. This disease fills the lungs with a thick fluid and makes breathing difficult. Jordan uses chemistry to study asthma. She hopes one day to find a cure for this disease.

Jordan prepared for her career by studying chemistry in college. She earned a bachelor's degree in chemistry at North Carolina Agricultural and Technical College in Greensboro, North Carolina. She then earned a doctoral degree in chemistry at MIT.

Lynda Jordan studies a protein called PLA_2 in her laboratory.

Lynda Jordan studies PLA$_2$ from human placentas.

Protein

Jordan studies protein. Protein is found in all living plant and animal cells. Cells need protein to function normally. But too much protein can have harmful effects.

Jordan studies a protein called PLA$_2$. She has learned this protein helps people fight off germs. PLA$_2$ also triggers normal childbirth.

But too much PLA_2 seems to be harmful. Jordan found high amounts of PLA_2 in people with asthma and diabetes. People with diabetes have too much sugar in their blood. Jordan hopes to find cures for asthma and diabetes.

In the past, scientists studied PLA_2 from snakes. Jordan began to study PLA_2 from human placentas. These organs are found in pregnant women. Food moves from the mother's body to the fetus through the placenta. A fetus is a human or an animal when it is developing in its mother's womb. The placenta also helps remove the fetus's waste. The placenta is pushed out of the woman's body after the baby is born.

Jordan studied the PLA_2 in placenta samples. She received placenta samples from hospitals. She carried the placentas to her laboratory in a special cooler. The cooler kept the placenta samples fresh so she could study PLA_2 in her laboratory.

Further Research

Jordan began teaching at North Carolina Agricultural and Technical College. But her laboratory there did not have the necessary equipment for research on PLA_2. Jordan then did research at a laboratory in Research Triangle Park near Raleigh, North Carolina. This laboratory was 55 miles (89 kilometers) from Greensboro. It had the necessary equipment for her research. But the placenta samples often spoiled in her car on the way to the laboratory.

Jordan was determined to keep studying PLA_2. She worked to get money from the federal government to do her research. The government gave her $1 million to build her own laboratory to study PLA_2.

Jordan received an award for her hard work and research. In 1995, First Lady Hillary Rodham Clinton presented Jordan with an award for Women in Science Technology and Engineering.

Jordan continues to study PLA_2. She hopes her research will lead to cures for diseases like asthma and diabetes.

Children with asthma often must take medicines to help them breathe.

Chapter 6

Malathy Nair

As a child in India, Malathy Nair often ate chapatis for breakfast. Chapatis are round, flat pieces of bread made from flour. Many Indian people eat chapatis. But chapatis do not provide people with certain necessary vitamins and minerals.

Today, Nair is a chemist. In her work, she makes food products from grain. These foods someday may help provide Indian people with many vitamins and minerals they need.

Nair prepared for her career by studying several subjects related to chemistry. She

Malathy Nair makes food products from grains.

first studied microbiology at the University of Bombay in India. Scientists in this field study living things that are too small to be seen without a microscope. Nair also studied biophysics at the university. Scientists in this field use matter and energy to try to solve problems with living things. Nair next studied food science. Nair earned a doctoral degree in food science from Rutgers University in New Brunswick, New Jersey.

Today, Nair works for the General Mills cereal company in Minneapolis, Minnesota. She uses her chemistry skills to create healthful cereals.

Food Science

Nair first worked as a chemist for a company in New Jersey that produced cooking oils. Restaurants sometimes use these oils to fry food. Some restaurants do not change their cooking oils as often as

Food scientists need good chemistry skills.

they should. Food cooked in overused oil can taste bad.

Nair invented a test to determine the freshness of cooking oils. Restaurants could use this test to quickly check their cooking oils. The test helped companies know when to replace their oils.

Nair worked to get her test approved by the U.S. government. This allowed restaurants and companies throughout the nation to use her test. She also worked to get laboratories throughout the world to try the test.

Grains and Cereals

At General Mills, Nair works with flours and grains. She makes cereals from different types of flours and grains to find out which foods make the best-tasting cereals. The company then uses these grains and flours to produce the cereals it sells in stores. Nair's

Malathy Nair makes cereals from grain products such as barley.

Malathy Nair tests cereals to make sure they are crisp.

work with flours and grains helps the company make cereals that taste good.

Nair tests cereals after they are made to make sure that they are crisp. Crisp cereals usually taste better. Baking changes the texture and flavor of cereals. Baking quickly can make cereals more crisp. Nair studies cereals to make sure workers at General Mills are baking them correctly.

In India, more people are buying products from the United States. In the past, people in India ate only breads and chapatis for breakfast. But today, Indian people also eat cereals. This means people in India now get many minerals, vitamins, and proteins from these grains. Nair hopes her cereals will help Indian people lead healthier lives.

Words to Know

asthma (AZ-muh)—a condition that causes people to have difficulty breathing

cell (SEL)—a microscopic part of a plant or animal

chapati (chuh-PAH-dee)—a flat, round wheat bread from India

diabetes (dye-uh-BEE-teez)—a disease in which there is too much sugar in the blood

donor (DOH-nur)—a person who agrees to give one of his or her organs to medical science to help sick people

fetus (FEE-tuhss)—a human or an animal when it is developing in its mother's womb

laboratory (LAB-ruh-tor-ee)—a room containing special equipment for people to use in scientific experiments

PLA$_2$ (PEE-EL-AY-TOO)—a protein that causes normal childbirth to occur; PLA$_2$ is found in human placentas.

placenta (pluh-SEN-tuh)—the organ found in a pregnant woman that feeds the fetus; the placenta also takes away the fetus's waste.

polymer (POL-uh-mur)—a natural or artificial material made of small parts linked together in long chains of repeating units; plastic is a polymer.

potpourri (poh-puh-REE)—a mixture of flowers, herbs, and spices that is kept in a jar and used for scent

protein (PROH-teen)—a substance found in all living plant and animal cells

transplant (TRANSS-plant)—an operation in which a diseased organ is replaced by a healthy one

To Learn More

Burns, George. *Exploring the World of Chemistry.* Try This. New York: Franklin Watts, 1995.

D'Amico, Joan and Karen Eich Drummond. *The Science Chef: 100 Fun Food Experiments and Recipes for Kids.* New York: J. Wiley & Sons, 1995.

Loeschnig, Louis V. *Simple Chemistry Experiments with Everyday Materials.* New York: Sterling Publishing, 1994.

Mebane, Robert C. and Thomas R. Rybolt. *Plastics and Polymers.* Everyday Material Science Experiments. New York: Twenty-First Century Books, 1995.

Newmark, Ann. *Chemistry.* Eyewitness Science. New York: DK Publishing, 1993.

Useful Addresses

The American Chemical Society
1155 16th Street NW
Washington, DC 20036

Association for Women in Science
1200 New York Avenue
Suite 650
Washington, DC 20005

**Society for Canadian Women in Science
  and Technology**
417-535 Hornby Street
Vancouver, BC V6C 2E8
Canada

Internet Sites

Comic Book Periodic Table
http://www.uky.edu/~holler/periodic/periodic.
  html

The Heart: An Online Exploration
http://sln2.fi.edu/biosci/heart.html

How Food Preservation Works
http://www.howstuffworks.com/
  food-preservation.htm

The Liver
http://tqjunior.advanced.org/4245/liver.htm

Understanding Our Planet
  through Chemistry
http://minerals.cr.usgs.gov/gips/aii-home.htm

Index